ATTACK OF THE ENDER DRAGON

ATTACK OF THE ENDER DRAGON

AN UNOFFICIAL MINETRAPPED ADVENTURE, #6

Winter Morgan

Sky Pony Press
New York

Copyright © 2016 by Hollan Publishing, Inc.

Minecraft® is a registered trademark of Notch Development AB.

The Minecraft game is copyright © Mojang AB.

Sky Pony Press books may be purchased in bulk at special discounts for sales
promotion, corporate gifts, fund-raising, or educational purposes. Special
editions can also be created to specifications. For details, contact the Special
Sales Department, Sky Pony Press, 307 West 36th Street, 11th Floor,
New York, NY 10018 or info@skyhorsepublishing.com.

Sky Pony® is a registered trademark of Skyhorse Publishing, Inc.®,
a Delaware corporation.

Minecraft® is a registered trademark of Notch Development AB.
The Minecraft game is copyright © Mojang AB.

Visit our website at www.skyponypress.com.

10 9 8 7 6 5 4 3 2 1

Library of Congress Cataloging-in-Publication Data is available on file.

Cover design by Brian Peterson
Cover photo by Megan Miller

Print ISBN: 978-1-5107-0602-6
Ebook ISBN: 978-1-5107-0612-5

Printed in Canada

TABLE OF CONTENTS

ATTACK OF THE ENDER DRAGON

1
TRY AGAIN

"I see it!" Simon called out.

"Great," Lily exclaimed. "Can you reach it?"

Michael looked at Simon and grabbed a pickaxe. "We'll have to mine to get it," he said.

Lily picked up her pickaxe and banged it against the blocky ground. "I see it too!"

The gang dug deep into the floor of the mine until Lily, Simon, and Michael were surrounded by blue.

Lily cried out, "Diamonds!"

"Sweet!" Michael exclaimed, and he grabbed as many diamonds as he could fit in his hands.

"This is the best mining job ever," Simon declared as he stuffed his inventory with diamonds.

"We should trade these at the blacksmith's shop and get more armor," Lily suggested.

"Good idea," Simon agreed as he scanned the mine. "I think we have all of them. Let's go back to Lisimi Village."

Blossom hurried into the mine. "Guess what, guys?"

"What is it, Blossom?" asked Lily.

"I think Mr. Anarchy has figured out the glitch. There are people crowded outside his lab." Blossom beamed.

"Wow," Simon exclaimed. "That's fantastic news."

"Is it true? How can we be sure? Maybe there is another reason people are at Mr. Anarchy's lab." Michael spit out a slew of questions. He was skeptical.

It had been a while since Sunny and the others were zapped off the server. Mr. Anarchy had come close to discovering why there was a glitch, but none of his attempts to solve it were successful, and Michael had been disappointed way too many times.

"I think this is it. I think it's real," Blossom told him.

"I hope so," Michael replied as he followed Blossom and the others back to Lisimi Village.

Simon remarked, "I've really enjoyed these last few months in Lisimi Village. It's a lot of fun to stay on this server when we aren't battling griefers."

The past few months had been peaceful, and the gang was able to explore the server. They had traveled to various biomes. One day they had an enormous snowball fight in the icy cold biome with all of the townspeople.

"Remember the snowball fight?" Lily recalled with a chuckle.

"I still have an inventory full of snowballs," Blossom gloated. "While you guys were busy pounding each other with frozen snowballs, I was collecting them."

"Why did you bother? It's not like anyone is going to spawn Nether mobs in the Overworld," Simon said. "We don't have any griefers to battle."

"You never know." Blossom defended her reasoning for hoarding snowballs, "I can use them when I'm in the Nether searching for treasure."

As the gang entered the village, Emily the Fisherwoman and Juan the Butcher approached them. Juan called out, "I think Mr. Anarchy has an announcement."

"We know!" Blossom replied, "I hope it's good news!"

"I think it is," Emily said. "I'm pretty sure he's found a way to get you guys back to the real world. There is a line forming outside his lab."

"Hope so!" Michael exclaimed. He was finally hopeful this would be the day he could go home.

Juan admitted, "I'll miss you guys."

"We'll try to come and visit like Pablo did," Lily told him, "but we'll miss you too. It's going to be hard trying to readjust to our old lives."

"You'll do fine," Emily said with a smile. "Go ahead and find out. Let us know."

The gang headed for Mr. Anarchy's lab. Although Lily had heard there was a long line outside his lab, she was still shocked when she saw it with her own eyes.

"Wow," Lily exclaimed, "look at how many people are waiting. It will take forever for everyone to get off the server."

"But we'll get off okay. I just know it," Blossom proclaimed.

Michael walked over to a townsperson standing in line and asked, "Is it true? Has Mr. Anarchy finally found a way to get us all home?"

The townsperson shrugged. "I'm not sure. Peter said Mr. Anarchy had a big announcement. Everyone raced over and once we got here, Peter told us to line up."

"Where is Peter?" Michael asked. He didn't see him on the line.

"I don't know. Nobody has seen Peter or Mr. Anarchy for a while. We've all been just standing in this line waiting."

"Really?" Michael began to worry.

Lily stood next to Michael and said, "I'm going to get some answers. I can't just stand here and wait." She entered the lab and called out, "Mr. Anarchy?"

There was no response.

Lily called out again, "Mr. Anarchy? Where are you?"

"In here." His voice was very faint.

Lily walked down a long dimly lit corridor. A pair of red eyes glared at her. She grabbed her diamond sword and struck the spider before it could inject her with any of its poison.

"Lily," Mr. Anarchy said as he ran toward her. "There you are. I'm having a bit of a problem."

"What happened?" asked Lily.

"I thought I found a way to get everyone off the server, but then I realized that it might not work. There is a line of people in front of my lab, and I don't want to disappoint them. I'm not sure how to let them know I made a mistake," confessed Mr. Anarchy.

"I knew it wouldn't work," a voice called out from behind them.

Lily turned around to see Michael approaching and she tried to explain his words to Mr. Anarchy. "Michael has been very sad lately. He keeps getting his hopes up and gets very upset when he's disappointed."

"I don't blame him," Mr. Anarchy said. "I'm upset with myself. I should have found a solution by now. I work tirelessly day and night, but I can't come up with any answers. It feels so pointless."

"No, it's not." Lily knew she had to give Mr. Anarchy a pep talk, but she didn't want to tell him to try harder because she knew he was trying as hard as he could. "You're doing your best. I know you feel it's impossible to solve this problem, but I have faith that you'll find a way to crack this code."

Mr. Anarchy smiled in appreciation. "You always make me feel better."

Lily continued to offer her support to Mr. Anarchy. "Maybe if you tell me what you're doing I can help."

"Okay." Mr. Anarchy rattled off the various ways he had worked with the command blocks to get every-one out of Lisimi Village and back to the real world.

Lily stood by the command blocks, listening to Mr. Anarchy's many stories about his failed experiments. Suddenly, they both heard a loud roar.

"What is that?" Lily gasped.

A scaly wing crashed into the lab and Mr. Anarchy leapt back, shielding himself from the rubble. "Oh no! It's the Ender Dragon!"

2

THE ATTACK OF THE ENDER DRAGON

Blossom aimed a hard icy snowball at the powerful dragon and it landed on the dragon's tail. Lily and Mr. Anarchy dashed from the lab, clutching their bows and arrows. Mr. Anarchy struck the beast with an arrow.

The crowd of townspeople scattered but they all attacked the flying beast with different weapons.

"Who summoned this dragon?" Lily cried out.

"Probably another griefer," Michael answered as he slammed his diamond sword into the beast. It roared in pain.

"We're weakening it." Simon was hopeful the dragon would be destroyed quickly.

Annihilating the dragon turned into a town effort, and with multiple strikes from diamond swords, snowballs, and arrows, the dragon was quickly losing its strength.

"We've got it!" Simon exclaimed as he delivered the final blow, obliterating the Ender Dragon.

The crowed cheered.

Michael stood emotionless. "We still don't know who summoned it. This isn't a time for celebrating. We have to figure out if there is a new griefer on the server."

"It could be a glitch," suggested Simon.

Mr. Anarchy interrupted the debate when he announced, "I'm sorry I made everyone wait, but I'm afraid I have some bad news. I thought I knew a way to get us off this server, but I encountered another glitch and my solution isn't working."

The crowd let out a collective moan.

Michael asked, "What happened?"

"It's hard to say, but just when it seemed I'd finally gotten to the root of the problem, I realized my problems had just begun." Mr. Anarchy apologized again and thanked everyone for their patience.

Peter also apologized. "I'm the one who spread the word around town and told you all to wait by Mr. Anarchy's lab. I'm sorry."

Robin hurried over to Lily. "Are you freaked out about the Ender Dragon?"

"Yes," Lily said. "I'm worried we could have a potential griefer on our hands. And since Mr. Anarchy announced he has no way to get us home, I can't take any more bad news. I want something happy to happen."

"Me too," Robin agreed.

Peter glanced at the sky. "It's getting dark. We should all head home for the night. Hopefully, Mr. Anarchy will make some progress with his project, and we can get back to the real world tomorrow."

Michael was annoyed with Peter. "You're filling everyone with false hope."

"Don't be such a downer," Peter said as he looked at Michael. "We're never going to succeed with that attitude."

The two stood face to face. Michael said, "I don't want to fight."

Peter said, "I know. Neither do I. I just want to get home."

Robin pointed to the nearby road and cried out, "Endermen!" Peter and Michael stopped arguing and sprinted toward Robin.

Six Endermen walked right by her; one shrieked and teleported. Robin ran as fast as she could to the shoreline.

Lily accidentally stared at one of the remaining Endermen, and another one unleashed a high-pitched cry and raced toward her. She rushed to the shore and jumped into the refreshing blue water alongside Robin. When the two were safely underneath the peaceful water, they heard a deafening roar.

"It can't be," Robin uttered as she came to the surface.

"Yes, it is," Lily gasped as another Ender Dragon flew boldly through the skies of Lisimi Village. "Who is summoning these beasts?" Robin was horrified.

"I have no idea." Lily grabbed her bow and arrow and tried to strike the dragon. The muscular beast was flying very fast, and Lily's arrow missed its scaly grey side.

Townspeople emerged from their homes and joined in the battle against the second Ender Dragon. Everyone was exhausted from waiting at Mr. Anarchy's lab and then being let down about the possible return to the real world. The dragon sensed the town's lack of energy and preyed on it. The beast roared and flew close to a group of people, knocking into them.

Blossom pulled another snowball from her inventory and slammed the ball into the dragon's side. It roared and she threw another icy ball.

"Good job, Blossom," Lily exclaimed as she moved to Blossom's side and aimed her bow and arrow.

"And you guys made fun of me for collecting snowballs," Blossom said as she struck the dragon again, and the beast lost another heart.

"You're right. If I had collected snowballs instead of taking part in the great snowball fight, I'd be in much better shape. But I have to admit, that snowball fight was a lot of fun," Lily replied as she shot another arrow and missed the dragon.

Blossom continued to pound the dragon with snowballs. Lily raced behind her, hoping one of her arrows would strike the dragon. She kept missing the dragon and was very annoyed at herself. Blossom struck the beast again.

The Ender Dragon let out a final roar. As the powerful dragon was destroyed, it dropped an egg and a portal to the End appeared.

Blossom grabbed the egg and stared at the portal. Michael walked over to her and warned, "Don't go to the End. Nobody likes the End, especially in real life."

Blossom shuddered. "I can't even imagine what it's like there," she said.

Lily wasn't contemplating a trip to the End, but was fixated on finding out who was summoning the Ender Dragon.

When Pablo appeared on the server, he stood beside Lily and asked, "What's going on? Have you encountered any Ender Dragons since Dylan left?"

"No, it's been quite peaceful," she answered.

Pablo shook his head. "That's strange."

Lily asked Pablo, "Do you know if there's another griefer on this server?"

"Not that I can tell," Pablo replied.

"There is definitely something strange going on," Robin said.

Lily looked up at the darkening sky and warned, "We have to get back to the cottage."

Pablo smiled. "Go home and be safe. I'll keep a watch on Lisimi Village."

As Lily and Robin hurried toward their house, they heard a thunderous boom. A lightning bolt flashed through the dark sky.

"Lily?" Robin cried.

Lily had vanished.

3
SURPRISE STORMS

"Lily!" Robin shouted out to her friend in the rain, but there was no response. The cottage door was open. Robin hoped Lily had rushed inside. She stepped into the small living room, calling her name, but there was still no response. Lily wasn't there.

Robin turned and headed back toward the door, ready to search for Lily in the dark stormy night, when four zombies entered the cottage. Robin reached for her sword, but she was outnumbered. The zombies extended their blocky arms, cornering her. She tried, but couldn't fight back. Robin respawned in her bed, and spotted the zombies lumbering toward her again. She was fumbling with her diamond sword when Lily dashed into the cottage, surprising the zombies and obliterating them.

"Lily!" Robin exclaimed.

Lily shut the cottage door. "I was zapped off."

"But you're back?"

"There must be a glitch. It was such an odd experience." Lily seemed out of sorts. She crawled into the bed beside Robin.

"What happened?"

Lily stuttered, "I'm n-not really sure. I was just gone and suddenly I was in the middle of Lisimi Village in the rain."

"So you didn't get back to the real world at all?"

"No, I just vanished and then reappeared. As I said, it was very odd." Lily spoke slowly, as if she was trying to process the entire experience.

"I know you're not going to like hearing me say this, but I'm glad you're back. I guess that's selfish of me, but I would be very lonely without you," Robin confessed.

"That's not selfish. I'd feel the same way if you were zapped off," Lily admitted, and she drifted off to sleep thinking about all of her friends who had left the server. It seemed like years since Greta and Brett had vanished with the Prismarines. She had so many friends who were able to escape, and she hoped she'd be the next one off.

The sun was shining the next morning and before Lily could get out of bed, Mr. Anarchy was at their door.

"Lily? Are you here?" Mr. Anarchy called.

"Yes," Lily replied and opened the door.

"I'm shocked. I heard Robin calling your name, " Mr. Anarchy exclaimed. "I thought you were zapped off last night. It was hard to sleep. I was worried I'd never see you again."

"You're right, I was zapped off, but there was a glitch and I didn't get there." Lily picked out cake from her inventory and offered a piece to Mr. Anarchy.

Mr. Anarchy thanked Lily for the cake and ate while pacing in the cottage living room. "I didn't summon that lightning bolt. It was a natural storm. This means it's not my lightning bolts that aren't working; it must be a problem with the server."

Robin climbed out of bed to have some cake. "Do you think someone is controlling the server?" she asked.

"That's the only thing that makes sense," Lily answered. "It might be the same person who spawned the Ender Dragon attacks."

Mr. Anarchy paused, swallowed his final bite of the cake and added, "I don't know about that. Now I'm wondering if there is a larger problem and if it might involve another griefer. But we can't be sure. I have to go back to my lab and get to work. I promise I will get to the bottom of this."

"I hope so," Lily replied and opened the door for Mr. Anarchy. She looked up at the cloudy sky and asked, "What happened to the sun?"

Robin went to the door, too, and studied the sky. "It's going to rain," she predicted.

More clouds filled the sky and soon rain started to fall on Lisimi Village. The morning storm was a breeding ground for hostile mobs. A horde of zombies spawned on the hillside, and a cluster of skeletons filled the narrow village streets, shooting arrows at anyone they encountered.

Warren sprinted toward the cottage. Lily watched him hurry through the rain, dodging arrows and avoiding zombie attacks. Just as he reached the front door, a lightning bolt struck him.

"Warren!" Lily, Robin, and Mr. Anarchy cried out in unison.

Warren was gone.

"I'm sure he'll respawn soon," Robin said.

The storm was intense. Zombies spawned and ripped doors from the villagers' homes. Lily searched through her inventory for potions to splash on the zombies, but she didn't have many left. "I wish Ilana was still on this server. I am running low on potions. Are there any other alchemists? Or are we going to have to brew our own potions?"

"I think we're going to have to brew our own potions," Robin replied, "but we don't have time to do that now. We have to fight. If you need any potions, you can always borrow them from me."

Mr. Anarchy still stood in the doorway waiting for the storm to pass. "I thought Warren would have respawned by now. This doesn't make any sense."

"Maybe the glitch is fixed," suggested Robin.

An army of zombies marched in the direction of the cottage. Lily cried, "I don't think we have time to analyze the glitch. We have to battle."

Lily put on her armor and fearlessly attacked the undead mob with her diamond sword.

4
GLITCHES

Lily was horrified as six zombies spawned clutching diamond swords. "This is going to be challenging," she exclaimed to Mr. Anarchy.

"Something is wrong with the coding on this server," he sighed, and then leaped at a vacant-eyed zombie holding a diamond sword.

One zombie slashed Robin's arm, and she cried out in pain. "These zombies are powerful. I'm losing hearts!"

"They're vicious," added Lily as she struck a zombie, but she was hurt when two zombies plunged their diamond swords into her legs.

Mr. Anarchy grabbed a potion of harming, splashing it on the beasts that were attacking them in the rain. Lily and Robin slammed their swords into the weakened zombies, obliterating three. As Mr. Anarchy battled the remaining three zombies, Robin and Lily rushed over to help him.

Mr. Anarchy used his final bottle of potion to weaken the three zombies, and Lily and Robin finally annihilated them.

"Looks like we're okay, for now," Lily said in relief.

"You spoke too soon. Look!" Robin gasped.

A second group of zombies lumbered toward them, outfitted in armor and holding swords.

"They have armor!" Lily cried.

"And swords!" Robin shrieked.

Mr. Anarchy's voice shook as he spoke "I don't have any potion left."

Robin scanned her inventory for a potion. She grabbed a bottle and dashed into the storm, splashing the armored zombies' heads.

"Help me!" Robin screamed in pain, as the zombies clobbered her.

"Did the potion work?" Lily called out as she struck the zombies, but they didn't lose any hearts.

More zombies wearing armor spawned in the distance. Mr. Anarchy's heart raced as he tried to destroy the current batch of zombies before the others approached. "I hope we can defeat these evil undead."

Three skeletons spotted the group battling the zombies and shot arrows at them. An arrow landed on Lily's arm, depleting her energy bar. She was destroyed and respawned in her bed, and then quickly ran toward the front door.

"Lily, are you okay?" Robin asked as she entered the room.

"What happened?" Lily questioned. "It's not raining?"

"Yes, the storm stopped," Robin explained. "Mr. Anarchy went back to his lab to figure out what is happening to this server."

"Did Warren respawn?" asked Lily.

"Not yet."

Lily and Robin walked into the town to search for their other friends. They were curious to see if anyone else had been zapped back to the real world during the storm.

Michael hurried over and told them, "I saw Warren get zapped off."

"And he hasn't respawned, which is a good sign," Lily remarked.

They heard a loud noise and saw a blue flash of light.

"That light and sound isn't a good sign!" Michael yelled.

A blue Wither spawned above Lisimi Village. Lily ducked into the library to shield herself from the wither skulls, but one hit her side, leaving her stuck with the Wither effect.

Simon spotted Lily in distress and rushed to her side with milk.

"Thanks," Lily mumbled. She was embarrassed that she was caught running into the library to avoid the Wither rather than fighting it.

"We can't run," Simon said, and he looked directly at Lily. "We have to battle this. We are so close to getting home."

Lily could see Michael and Robin tirelessly battling the tricky Wither; she felt a pang of guilt. How could she abandon her friends? "But I have just battled armored, sword-carrying zombies," Lily protested.

"So did I." Simon handed Lily a snowball and took her by the arm. "Come with me," he encouraged, "we'll win this battle together." The duo raced to their friends' side, fighting the Wither alongside them.

Blossom dashed into the town loaded up with snowballs. The Wither was unusually weak, and Lily was surprised at how effortless it seemed to battle this challenging flying terror. The Wither exploded, dropping a Nether star.

"You can have the Nether star," Michael told Blossom. "Your endless supply of snowballs has been very handy."

"Thanks," Blossom said, and she placed the Nether star in her inventory.

"You deserve it," Michael replied with a smile.

"I wish the star was powerful enough to get me home," commented Blossom.

Suddenly, they heard Mr. Anarchy scream from his lab, "I've got it! I've got it!"

Michael grinned at Blossom. "Maybe you just got your wish."

"I don't think the Nether star is powerful enough to get me home," Blossom replied.

The gang rushed to Mr. Anarchy's lab eager to hear what he had discovered.

"What's going on?" Lily asked as she strolled into the lab.

Mr. Anarchy was in the back room, but a person with red hair, wearing a yellow shirt and jeans, approached Lily and questioned, "Who are you? . . . and where am I?"

"In Lisimi Village," Lily informed him.

"Where is that? Am I in Minecraft for real?" He was disoriented and asked, "What's happening?"

Mr. Anarchy emerged from the back room of the lab. Lily was angry and started to interrogate him. "Did you zap a new person on to the server? How can you do that? You said you'd never do that again. What's wrong with you?"

The red-headed man stood silently as Mr. Anarchy tried to calm down Lily. "I didn't zap him on—"

Lily interrupted Mr. Anarchy and raised her voice. "Really?"

"Please let me finish. I meant I didn't do it on purpose. I was trying to sort out the glitch and I was trying all sorts of experiments and this one involved seeing if I could zap someone on."

"Why would you conduct an experiment like that?" pressed Lily.

"I had to conduct all types of experiments. Now I know that I still have the power to zap people from this server into the game, which gives me hope that I can zap people off again."

Lily listened, but she was still angry. As she looked at the innocent man who stood in the dimly lit corner of Mr. Anarchy's lab, she spotted a pair of red eyes peering out from behind him. She grabbed her sword and lunged at the spider, but the man was confused and thought Lily was attacking him.

"What?" he cried out and grabbed a sword.

"I'm sorry," Lily tried to explain, but she was busy pounding her sword against the creepy spider. "There was a spider behind you. I didn't have time to warn you. I had to destroy it before you were poisoned."

"Thank you, I guess," the man replied.

Mr. Anarchy said, "I'm sorry I zapped you into the game. I will try to get you back home as quickly as I can."

"What is your name?" asked Lily.

"Oscar," he said quietly.

"Hi, Oscar. I'm Lily," she said with a smile. "It's going to be okay. You came at a good time. We are just figuring out how to leave here."

"I don't want to be here at all," Oscar demanded. "Send me home now."

"I'm afraid I can't do that," Mr. Anarchy explained.

"Mr. Anarchy," Lily informed him, "there is a crowd of people outside waiting for you to make an announcement again. Everyone heard you exclaim "I've got it" and they think you've finally discovered the glitch."

"What am I going to tell them? Look at how upset you were when you discovered I zapped Oscar on to the server. They might attack me. I'm so nervous." Mr. Anarchy's heart raced.

Thunder boomed outside, and Lily headed for the exit. Oscar followed closely behind her as a lightning bolt flashed in front of them. Oscar vanished. Mr. Anarchy was relieved, but when the storm ended, he'd still have to answer questions from the townspeople.

On the other side of town, another lightning bolt struck Peter.

"Peter!" Michael called out, as the clouds disappeared and the sun came out.

5
BACK TO THE LAB

"Is Peter coming back?" Michael searched the grassy area in front of Mr. Anarchy's lab in hopes of finding his friend.

"No," Mr. Anarchy replied, "I think he's back in the real world just like Warren."

The townspeople crowded around Mr. Anarchy as he spoke. They interrupted him, asking him questions about getting zapped back to the real world: "Have you discovered the glitch? Can you get us home? Is there another griefer that's spawning the Ender Dragon?"

"I'm not sure I can answer all of your questions," Mr. Anarchy stated nervously. "I didn't have anything to do with Warren and Peter getting zapped off the server."

"Who was the man with the red hair?" one townsperson questioned.

"He was accidentally zapped onto the server," Mr. Anarchy confessed.

"Accidentally?" another townsperson called out.

Mr. Anarchy started to shake when a townsperson wailed, "He's a griefer again. Mr. Anarchy is a griefer."

Lily stood in the center of town and defended her friend. "He is not a griefer. He's working with us and we'll all get zapped off soon."

Another townsperson called out to Mr. Anarchy, "Prove you're not a griefer. I want you to zap someone off right now."

Mr. Anarchy didn't know if he could pull this off, but he knew he had to try. He ordered, "Everyone write your name on a slip of paper and place it on the ground."

The townspeople followed his orders. Mr. Anarchy asked Michael to choose a name from the pile on the ground as he excused himself with, "I'm going inside to summon the lightning bolt."

Michael leaned down and picked up a name. His eyes filled with tears when he read the name aloud, "Lily."

Mr. Anarchy didn't hear Lily's name called. He was already in his lab working on the command blocks, trying to successfully summon a lightning bolt to zap the chosen person off the server, so he wouldn't be attacked by the townspeople. He worked very carefully as he summoned the bolt and then hurried outside to see if it had worked.

"Lily!" Simon called out.

"She's gone," Michael said as he looked at Mr. Anarchy.

The crowd let out a collective cheer. Mr. Anarchy's lightning bolt had worked and Lily was back home.

"I want to go next," one of the villagers called out.

Mr. Anarchy looked down at the ground. He couldn't answer. He was devastated that Lily was gone. "I'm glad it worked," he sniffled.

"Now we can all get home," Michael said to cheer up Mr. Anarchy, but it was hard. He also was sad about Lily leaving Lisimi Village.

Robin smiled. "I miss her, but I'm happy for Lily."

Simon wondered aloud, "Will she tell my parents that I'm here? They must be so worried."

Before anyone had a chance to respond, Pablo appeared in the center of Lisimi Village.

"Pablo," Michael rushed over to him. "Have you heard anything about Lily?"

"Yes," Pablo replied. "She made it back to the real world. I've already sent her a message explaining how to enter this server as a player without getting zapped on. It's quite tricky. I know Warren was having issues signing on."

"Warren is safe, too?" asked Simon.

"Yes," Pablo said as he walked over to Mr. Anarchy. "I think this is your chance to get everyone off the server."

"I know," Mr. Anarchy replied, but he worried it wouldn't work. There was something unpredictable about this server, and he wasn't completely confident.

Pablo added, "I can tell there's something on the server that's making it have glitches. There are times I can't get on to this server at all. It's very frustrating."

"That's true," Mr. Anarchy agreed with Pablo, and he walked back into his lab to work on the command blocks.

Suddenly, there was a loud explosion. *Kaboom!*

Mr. Anarchy flew out of the lab. "It's my lab! Someone destroyed all of the command blocks with TNT."

Michael was furious. "Who would do that?" he shouted.

"It has to be someone here." Simon glared at the townspeople.

"It can't be." Robin was so shocked she questioned, "Who would want to trap us here?"

A tearful Blossom wailed, "Now we'll never get home."

Mr. Anarchy didn't want this to break him. He had suffered losses before and had always come back strong. Fortunately, there was one person who believed in him and led him to his small victories. That was Lily. Without her, Mr. Anarchy felt lost.

Mr. Anarchy mustered up enough strength to address the crowd: "We need command blocks. If anyone has some for me, I will begin to summon the lightning bolts."

As the townspeople searched through their inventories, a voice called out from the crowd.

"Mr. Anarchy!" the voice called.

"Lily?" Mr. Anarchy smiled.

6

HOMESICK

Lily met up with her friends Michael and Simon. "I can't talk now, guys. I was zapped home, but we're in the middle of the storm. When everything is settled, I'll contact you. But hopefully you'll be back in the real world soon." Lily then disappeared.

Pablo said, "I'm going to go, too."

"Is there a storm by you?" asked Blossom.

"No," Pablo clarified, "when you get zapped back, you enter the real world at the same minute you left. I arrived later though, and that is probably because I live in another part of the world. That's the cool thing about these types of servers. They connect people from across the globe and we can communicate with each other."

Blossom said, "I never thought about that. You're right. We might all be from different parts of the world, but in Lisimi Village, we're all the same."

Pablo excused himself. "My little sister needs the computer for her schoolwork. I have to go."

Pablo vanished, but as he disappeared another explosion was heard in the distance.

"What is that?" Blossom cried.

"It sounds like it's coming from the center of town," Michael exclaimed.

Everyone rushed into town to see what was damaged. Juan the Butcher raced over to them, his eyes swollen with tears. "The library! Our precious library! Someone destroyed it!"

"Who would do that?" Michael was devastated.

"I don't know," Juan cried out.

Emily the Fisherwoman hurried over. "Luckily, the librarian wasn't in there or it would have been even worse."

"Who is blowing up all of these places in Lisimi Village? First, we watched the lab get blown up and now the library," noted Robin. While she spoke she thought about potential suspects, but couldn't come up with any names.

Michael said, "It has to be someone who wants us trapped on this server."

"Or someone who doesn't want to leave," added Simon.

"That's insane. Who wouldn't want to leave this server?" questioned Michael.

Robin wondered if Dylan had returned like Pablo and Lily had and was terrorizing them. "Next time we see Pablo and Lily, we have to ask them about Dylan. Maybe he's back."

"I don't even want to think about that," Blossom said.

Mr. Anarchy was listening to everyone's theories. He didn't even care to find out who was destroying Lisimi Village. He just wanted to leave the server and get back home. They had overstayed their welcome in Lisimi Village and it was his fault. He knew that he was responsible for everyone being trapped on the server, and he just wanted to get the people off.

"We need to get off this server," Mr. Anarchy shouted, surprising everyone.

"I know," Michael agreed.

"I still need more command blocks."

The townspeople searched their inventories and gathered command blocks. They handed the blocks to Mr. Anarchy, and he placed them in his inventory. "I have to rebuild the lab next."

Robin suggested, "Why don't you work in the cottage? Now that Lily is back in the real world, there's room for you."

Mr. Anarchy contemplated this idea. He did miss Lily an incredible amount and would love to work on the command blocks while living in her space. The cottage reminded him of Lily, and it brought a smile to his face. "Yes, I'd love to stay in the cottage."

"Great," Robin replied, "then it's confirmed."

Michael paced outside Mr. Anarchy's lab. He peeked inside and looked at the rubble. "We still don't know who destroyed this place. I don't feel safe in Lisimi Village anymore."

Simon spoke his opinion to Michael. "I think someone wants us to stay trapped on this server."

Michael nodded and suggested, "While Mr. Anarchy works on the command blocks at the cottage and tries to get us all off the server, why don't we solve the mystery of who is blowing up Lisimi Village?"

"Deal," Simon smiled and high-fived his friend.

Mr. Anarchy followed Robin back to the cottage. As he entered the small house, he thought he could hear Lily's voice, but he knew he was just imagining things.

"You can work on the command blocks over here," Robin said as she cleared a space for Mr. Anarchy in the cozy living room.

Mr. Anarchy gazed out the picture window at the peaceful blue water. "Lily really constructed a nice cottage."

"Do you miss Lily?" Robin asked.

"Yes," he replied, "can't you tell?"

"Me too," Robin said. She wondered if she could be of any help and asked, "Is there any way I can help you with the command blocks? I'd love to help everyone get off the server as quickly as possible."

"Sure," Mr. Anarchy replied, and he explained how he used the command blocks.

While Mr. Anarchy and Robin worked on the blocks, Michael and Simon patrolled Lisimi Village.

Michael rattled off places he was worried might explode. "What about Juan's butcher shop?"

Simon shook his head. "I guess so. But why there?"

"It's a great resource for us, and Juan is very active in Lisimi Village. He's always helping us when there's a griefer bothering our town," Michael said.

"I'm not sure Juan's butcher shop is a target." Simon walked through the village streets searching for TNT. "We have to keep looking. I don't want to miss any TNT bricks that someone might have placed in the village."

"I just wish we knew what they are planning to blow up next." Michael wasn't enjoying playing the role of sleuth; he wanted answers and he wanted them now.

Pablo appeared in the village. "Hey guys, I'm here," he called out. My sister is done with her school project."

Michael asked, "Have you heard from Lily?"

"No," Pablo replied. "I saw her the same time you did. I'm sure she's stuck at home in the storm."

"Yeah," Simon said, "that storm was very intense. I'll bet she doesn't even have power."

Pablo asked, "What are you guys doing?"

Michael explained that they were searching for the culprit who was blowing up random spots in town. Pablo said, "Wow, I hope you find the person responsible." He excused himself again because it was dinnertime at home.

As Pablo faded, there was another explosion.

Michael shuddered and hollered, "It sounds like it's coming from the direction of the cottage!"

7
MISSING

Michael and Simon rushed to the cottage, calling out for Mr. Anarchy and Robin, but they heard nothing.

"Where are they?" Michael was frantic.

"I don't know," Simon replied as he stepped over the rubble littering the living room floor. "I can't find them."

"The townspeoples' command blocks are destroyed." Michael stared at the floor in disbelief.

"Robin!" Simon hollered, but it was pointless. He had called her name out numerous times and there hadn't been a response.

"This has to be the work of someone who wants us to stay on this server," Michael theorized.

Simon agreed, "Yes, it looks like the person who is doing this is picking his targets wisely."

"I'm not sure why they destroyed the library, but I'll bet if we go back there, we might get some answers," suggested Michael.

The duo headed for the library. As the sky grew dark, Simon noted, "This has to be a quick trip. It's almost nighttime."

Michael pointed to the library in the distance. "I think we have time to check it out before any hostile mobs spawn."

Arriving there in just minutes, Simon climbed through the crumbled library's façade, searching for any clues. There were aisles of books and piles of rubble, but they couldn't find anything that might help them.

Michael browsed through the books. "I don't see any enchanted books or anything."

Simon called out, "Over here!"

Michael rushed over to Simon who stood by a chest. "I wonder who left this chest."

Simon opened the chest and announced, "It's empty."

Michael peered through a hole in the library wall. "It's getting very dark. We have to head back to my house quickly."

Simon and Michael jogged all the way from the library and were inches from Michael's house when four block-carrying Endermen walked past them. One of the lanky Endermen made eye contact with Simon and unleashed a high-pitched shriek. Simon began to sprint toward the shoreline but it was too late. The Enderman attacked him first.

Simon fumbled, trying to get his sword from his inventory. The Enderman attacked Simon again and he lost a heart.

"Help!" he called out, but Michael was busy battling three Endermen.

Simon finally grabbed his diamond sword and slammed it into the Enderman, but he was too weak to continue the battle. Simon was destroyed and respawned in his bed.

Simon looked out the window. It was pitch-dark and he wasn't sure what had happened to Michael. He knew that it was too dangerous to search for him and crawled back into bed. Simon hoped they would get answers in the morning.

The sun shone through the small window, waking Simon up. He groggily pulled the covers off and climbed out of bed when he heard Michael calling his name.

"Michael," Simon said, "I'm here."

"Good," Michael replied, "I'm here with Blossom."

Blossom spoke rapidly and appeared quite nervous. "I can't believe Mr. Anarchy is missing. Now we'll never get off the server."

Simon took a piece of cake from his inventory and offered it to Blossom. She accepted and munched on the cake.

"We can't worry too much, that's not going to help us at all. We have to solve the problem and figure out how to get off this server," advised Simon.

Blossom was doubtful. "Do you think we have the capability of getting off this server on our own?"

Michael replied, "I don't know, but we're going to have to try. If we can't find Robin and Mr. Anarchy we'll have no choice."

Blossom's eyes filled with tears. "What if Robin and Mr. Anarchy are back in the real world? I feel like everyone is back there except us. Sunny, Lily, Peter, Ilana . . ." Blossom barely finished the list of all their friends who had gotten back to the real world because of her sobbing.

"We will be next," Simon reassured her. "Michael and I are gathering clues." He told Blossom about the chest they discovered in the library.

"But what does that mean?" questioned Blossom.

Simon didn't have a chance to reply. Six creepers silently crept into his living room and exploded behind Blossom, destroying her. Michael and Simon hurried to Blossom's house. They didn't want her to be alone when she respawned. As they entered her house, Blossom appeared in her bed. She jumped up and asked, "Who is the griefer?"

"I don't know," Simon replied, "but we'll find out."

Blossom asked about Mr. Anarchy and Robin. "Do you think they're in Mr. Anarchy's lab?"

Simon felt foolish. They had never checked the lab. "You might be right."

The gang dashed over to the lab, but it was empty. A few spiders crawled down the dirt hallway.

Michael destroyed them with a strike from his diamond sword.

"There's nothing here," Simon said in disappointment, "so we should leave."

"Wait, I think I see something," Blossom called out.

8
NEW ENEMY

"What is it? What do you see?" Michael questioned as he rushed toward Blossom.

"It's just an empty chest," Blossom groaned when she lifted the lid. "I thought it might be full of something valuable."

"That's the second empty one we found," Simon remarked. "I think there isn't anything worthwhile left to search here. Let's go back to the cottage and see if we missed anything."

Winding their way to the cottage, they noted that the town was desolate. Most people were staying in their homes. They were afraid because of the explosions and the sudden attacks from the Ender Dragon.

The trio felt very alone because most of their friends had gotten off the server. Michael hoped Robin and Mr. Anarchy would be in the cottage, but when they arrived, it was still empty.

As they entered the cottage, Blossom reminded them, "We have to watch out for creepers." Michael stood in the living room, trying to see if there was anything he overlooked the last time they searched. "It looks as if the person knew where Mr. Anarchy was using the command blocks and left the TNT right outside this area." Michael poked his head through a hole in the wall to check everywhere.

Blossom headed into Robin and Lily's bedroom. "If Robin was destroyed in the blast, she could have respawned in her bed. It isn't damaged at all."

"I'll bet she's still on this server," Simon said as he stared at the bed.

"Maybe they're trapped," Blossom suggested.

"I hope not," Simon replied.

"We have to find them," Michael concluded.

A voice called out from the living room, "Michael! Simon!"

Michael went to follow the sound of the voice and found Pablo waiting there. "Pablo," Simon asked, "has Lily returned any of your messages?"

"No," Pablo replied, "I'm sorry."

"That's okay," Simon said. "I'm sure we'll hear from her soon. I really thought she would have visited by now."

Pablo questioned, "What are you guys doing in here? Is everything okay?"

"No, it's not. After you left last night, the cottage exploded." Michael pointed to the hole in the wall.

"And Robin and Mr. Anarchy are missing," added Blossom.

"Really?" Pablo appeared shocked.

"Yes, we thought they'd be here." Michael was upset.

Pablo sighed. "I feel for you guys. I hated being on this server. Being home is the greatest. Yesterday my parents took me out to a restaurant and I ate French fries. I know you guys have potatoes, but French fries are so much better."

"Stop talking about home," Blossom said. She was so annoyed. "Are you trying to make us feel worse? None of us want to be trapped on this server. And we all miss French fries."

"Sorry," Pablo said, "I forget sometimes that you are trapped."

Michael walked over to Blossom to cheer her up. "We're going to get off this server soon. I promise."

"Yeah, I hope you do," Pablo said and then excused himself. "Gotta go, my dad needs to use the computer. See you later."

The minute Pablo disappeared they heard another explosion. Blossom cried out, "We have to find out what exploded this time."

Michael didn't move. He just shook his head. "I think I know who the griefer is."

"Me too," Simon said and asked, "Do you think it's Pablo?"

"Why Pablo?" questioned Blossom.

"Every time he shows up, something explodes," explained Michael.

Blossom thought for a moment and surmised, "He did brag about the French fries."

"What can we do?" Simon asked. "He's in the real world. We can't destroy him. He's just playing the game and we're stuck in it."

Blossom started to panic. "This is awful! Now it will be even harder to get home. We have to battle a person who is way too powerful!"

Michael said, "If we just find Robin and Mr. Anarchy, I'm sure we'll find the answers we need."

"But where are they?" Blossom cried.

Simon suggested they head to town to ask people if they had seen them. The others agreed and the gang walked to the demolished library. There they spotted Fred the Farmer.

"Can you believe somebody destroyed our nice library?" Fred said as he stood by the old entrance.

"And the blacksmith's shop," Juan the Butcher added.

"Who would blow up the blacksmith shop?" questioned Blossom.

"Someone who doesn't want us to replenish our supply of weapons," suggested Simon.

"Who would cause all of this devastation?" Juan asked. He was upset, too.

"I'm sure it's the same person who blew up the cottage and Mr. Anarchy's lab," Michael said. He asked Fred and Juan if they had seen Robin and Mr. Anarchy.

"I saw Robin," Fred replied, "and she looked very upset."

"When did you see her?" Michael asked.

"It was just a few minutes ago," he told them. "I was picking some carrots on my farm when she walked by. She was crying. I asked her if she was okay, but she didn't respond."

"Which direction did she go?" asked Blossom.

"She was headed in the direction of the jungle biome." Fred pointed off to a grassy hill.

"We need to go find her," Simon exclaimed.

Michael, Simon, and Blossom hurried off toward the jungle biome. They didn't have a map or any idea where they were going, but they were hopeful that Robin was still on the server.

"Where can she be?" Simon felt frustrated as they roamed through the jungle biome and Robin was still nowhere to be seen. The gang circled the entire area. Huge green leaves shaded the jungle path. Simon searched for any sign of a jungle temple. He knew Robin had to be somewhere in the jungle.

Blossom called out when she spotted the walls of a jungle temple, "Over there! Maybe she's inside."

The moss and cobblestone temple was hidden behind enormous trees full of cocoa beans.

Blossom stopped abruptly and pointed. "There's an ocelot!"

"We don't have time to tame an ocelot now," Simon told her.

The muscular animal bounded through the leafy biome, disappearing into the lush landscape.

The gang continued down the path toward the temple. Blossom entered first and searched the ground floor, calling out, "Robin."

Michael searched for hidden treasure, but the temple had already been looted. "It looks like someone got to the treasure before we did."

"Do you think that's a sign?" asked Blossom. "Do you think Robin took the treasure?"

Simon heard a voice and asked the others, "Do you hear that?"

The gang stood silently, but they couldn't hear anything but the leaves blowing in the wind.

"I think you're imagining things, Simon," Blossom said.

"What if someone is going to attack us?" Simon was worried.

"We can escape on the river," Michael reminded him. "This jungle is so dense with trees, we can cut wood quickly and craft boats."

"That's a good plan," Simon said.

"And I don't hear a voice at all," Blossom said. She wondered why they were bothering to come up with a plan of escape when they weren't even being attacked.

"No, I definitely heard a voice," Simon insisted. He was sure he had heard someone talking. "Can't you guys hear it?"

Blossom stood quietly and listened but she couldn't hear anything. "What did they say?" she asked.

"I think someone is calling my name." Simon was getting irritated. "I can't be the only person who can hear it."

"Where is it coming from?" Blossom asked. Simon didn't answer her.

Michael said, "I'm going to search the rest of this temple for clues. We have to find something here." Michael checked the rest of the jungle temple and was excited when he spotted another empty chest. He called his friends over, but they didn't respond. When he went to look for Simon and Blossom, he was shocked to see them talking to someone.

Michael gasped, "Lily! Is that really you?"

9
COMPUTER PROBLEMS

"Yes, it's me," Lily said, "but I don't think I can stay on the server too long. It has a lot of glitches."

"We think Pablo is griefing this server," Michael blurted out.

"You're right," Lily replied. "He is."

"How do you know?" Blossom was utterly shocked by Lily's reply.

"He—" Lily vanished before she could finish her sentence.

"Lily!" Simon gasped.

"I had so many questions I wanted to ask her," groaned Michael. Her disappearance upset him. "But I have to tell you guys something. I found another empty chest."

"Does that make this place a target?" questioned Blossom.

"I hope not, but there's no reason to stick around here. We have to find Robin," Michael replied.

"Which way should we go?" Blossom asked as they exited the jungle temple. She stopped outside the temple's cobblestone steps and picked a melon. "There are so many ripe melons in this jungle biome, we should take a few."

Michael and Simon were running low on food, so they agreed to pick melons with Blossom. They stopped when a voice called out in the distance.

"Lily?" Blossom asked, tingling with excitement.

They couldn't see anyone through the heavy screen of leaves, but the unknown person called out again.

The voice asked, "Is anyone there?"

Simon hurried toward the sound of the voice. "It's Robin!" he cried out.

The trio was thrilled to be reunited with Robin, but the joyous reunion was cut short when a loud roar boomed throughout the verdant jungle.

"It can't be!" Robin cried.

The Ender Dragon unleashed another deafening roar and lunged at the gang. Blossom threw an endless number of snowballs, striking the side of the grey beast, while Robin, Simon, and Michael shot arrows at the dragon.

Michael grabbed a pickaxe, pounding it into a redwood tree. Simon was puzzled at his friend's action. "Dude, what are you doing? We have to fight the Ender Dragon."

"Let's just get out of here. We can build a boat to save ourselves," Michael defended his plan.

"The beast will just fly to the next biome, you know that. There's no escaping the Ender Dragon," Simon countered.

The dragon flew at Michael, striking him. The powerful blow from the Ender Dragon left Michael's health bar depleted. He didn't have time to trade his pickaxe for a sword; he was struck by the dragon and was destroyed.

Blossom continued to bombard the dragon with snowballs. "There are only four of us. This isn't going to be easy," she called out as she watched Michael disappear.

Robin ran right up close to the winged enemy and doused it with a potion. The dragon screamed in pain as it lost a heart.

Simon aimed his bow and arrow at the flying menace. "Bull's-eye," he exclaimed as he hit the beast four times.

Michael reappeared almost immediately. "I teleported," he said as he grabbed his sword and lunged at the dragon, delivering the final blow.

Blossom grabbed the egg the dragon had dropped and everyone avoided the portal to the End.

Simon nervously watched the sky and asked, "Do you think another one will spawn?"

Robin replied, "We have to get back to Mr. Anarchy. He'll know what to do."

"Do you know where he is?" questioned Simon.

"Yes, I do." Robin told them what happened after the house exploded. "After we were destroyed by TNT, I respawned in the bed and Mr. Anarchy must have respawned in his bed. I went out to look for him, and when I showed up at the lab, Pablo appeared. He told me Mr. Anarchy was in the jungle, because Pablo had found command blocks there. I teleported to Mr. Anarchy and we quickly built a house, since it was nighttime and we didn't want to be destroyed."

"Did Pablo go to the jungle with you?" asked Simon.

"No." Robin took a deep breath as she continued with her story. "He had to leave the server because it was dinnertime."

"I'll bet he was going to eat French fries," Michael sneered.

"What did you say?" asked Robin.

"Nothing," Michael muttered.

"We spent the night in a small house in the jungle. In the morning, we searched for the command blocks Pablo had told us about, but we couldn't find them. We found this stronghold filled with empty chests. Neither of us had any torches left in our inventory and the dark stronghold was a breeding ground for skeletons. We tried to search for the skeleton spawner, but we were constantly being destroyed by skeletons. It was a pointless and really exhausting battle."

"Where is Mr. Anarchy now?" asked Michael.

"The last time I was destroyed, I went back to the stronghold, but I didn't see him. I left to search for him, and that's when I found you guys," explained Robin.

A voice called out in the distance, "Guys!"

"Is that Lily?" Robin was utterly stunned.

10
SCUFFLE WITH SKELETONS

Lily was having a hard time getting onto the server. The connection was spotty, and her computer kept freezing up, so she could only access the server for a couple of seconds. The storm had passed through the town, knocking the electricity out for a few hours, but luckily her laptop was fully charged. She wanted to call her friends to see if they too were back in the real world, but she knew she wouldn't be able to reach them. She felt out of sorts being back in the real world without them, but also because time moved very slowly in the real world. They had been on the server for days, while only a couple of hours had passed in the real world. When she logged in and got onto the server, she found her friends in the jungle, but the minute she called out to them, she was shut off the server. Lily was devastated. She wanted to talk to Robin and she wanted to find Mr. Anarchy.

"Not again!" she yelled, and her mother asked her if everything was okay.

"Yes," she replied quickly, not wanting to alert her mother to what was happening in the world of Minecraft.

Robin watched as Lily vanished from the server. "Lily!" she cried.

Simon could hear a voice in the distance. "Quiet!" he said to Robin, "I think I hear Mr. Anarchy."

"Where is it coming from?" Robin looked through a thick patch of leaves; she could hear the voice, but wasn't sure which direction to go.

"I think he's over here," Blossom called out and ran down a grassy path lined with trees.

"That's near the stronghold," Robin told them. "I can show you the entrance." Robin led them to a hole in a large redwood tree. "In here."

The gang followed Robin into the tree. She called out, "Mr. Anarchy? Are you in here?"

"Robin," she heard. His voice was faint.

Blossom cried out in pain and grabbed her arm. Three arrows pierced her body and she started losing hearts. "Skeletons!" Blossom was struck by four more arrows and narrowly dodged another barrage as she grabbed milk from her inventory to replenish her energy.

Robin struck two skeletons with her diamond sword as she called out for her lost friend, Mr. Anarchy, but there was no response. Robin worried that he had been destroyed by the skeletons and had respawned in the jungle house. She wanted to escape from the skeleton battle and search for Mr. Anarchy in the jungle, but more skeletons spawned and she couldn't leave the battle. In fact, she could barely keep up with the bony beasts, which outnumbered her friends.

Michael and Simon splashed potions on the skeletons. Michael cried out, "I have to search for the spawner. It's the only way we can win this battle."

"I think it's in the dungeon," Robin shouted.

"I'm going there right now," Michael hollered and he sprinted toward the dungeon, leaving his friends to finish the battle with the horde of skeletons.

Michael dodged two skeletons walking down the hall, avoiding a strike from the hostile mob. As he made his way down to the dungeon, he could hear the rattling of skeleton bones and was terrified when he approached the spawner. He wasn't sure he could destroy the spawner on his own. Michael grabbed his iron pickaxe and banged the spawner. It wasn't easy. He used all of his strength and was barely able to demolish the skeleton spawner, but he finally destroyed it. Michael rushed back to his friends.

He entered the stronghold and called out to them, "Simon, Robin, Blossom!"

There was no reply. Nobody was there.

"Guys?" shouted Michael, "Where are you?"

Pablo appeared in the stronghold.

Michael was annoyed to see him. "What do you want? I know you are the one causing all of this trouble. Why would you do that to us? I don't understand.

You are back home and have all the comforts of real life. Why would you want to trap us here?"

Pablo chuckled. "I don't want to hurt you guys. Why would you think that?"

"Don't lie to me," Michael replied. He wanted to threaten Pablo with his diamond sword but he knew it was pointless. Pablo could be destroyed a million times and it wouldn't matter at all. To Pablo, this was just a game, but to Michael, this was real life.

"I'm not lying. Why would you think I'm a griefer?" asked Pablo. "Just because I griefed on the server before I was zapped off doesn't mean I am doing it from the real world."

Michael listed all of the reasons he suspected Pablo. "Every time you show up there is a TNT explosion."

"That can be just a coincidence," Pablo defended himself.

Michael was about to tell Pablo that Lily had confirmed that Pablo was a griefer, but before he could speak, Lily spawned in front of them.

"Lily!" Michael said with a smile.

"Lily," Pablo frowned.

"Where are the others?" Lily asked them.

They replied in unison, "I don't know."

"Pablo," she said as she stepped right up to him and held her diamond sword against his chest, which was more for effect than for action. "I can't believe you. Leave them alone. I know your secrets."

"What secrets?" Pablo questioned.

"I have the emails you sent," she yelled. "Do you want me to read them to Michael?"

Pablo didn't respond. He vanished.

"What did he write in the emails?" Michael was curious.

"It doesn't matter," Lily replied. "We have to find the others quickly."

Lily hurried out of the stronghold and Michael followed closely behind her. "Where do you think they are?" he asked.

"I'm not sure," she answered, as she sheared a path through the lush jungle biome.

"I hear voices," Michael told her, and he strained to listen.

"Me too!" Lily exclaimed.

Michael was a step behind Lily when she vanished. "Lily!" he called out, but there was no response.

The voices grew louder, and Michael panted as he raced toward them. He could see Robin and Blossom through a patch of leaves.

"Guys!" Michael exclaimed, "I'm over here!"

"It's Michael," Mr. Anarchy cried.

A shattering blast shook the jungle. Trees fell all over. Michael couldn't see his friends.

11

YOU CAN'T TAKE IT WITH YOU

"**G**uys!" Michael cried out again, jumping over fallen trees.

"Michael," Simon's faint voice called to his friend, "we're over here by the house."

Michael ran to his friends, grabbing a potion from his inventory and handing it to them. "You need to get your energy back."

"That's true," Simon said as he sipped the potion and thanked his friend.

"I don't have any potions left," Robin confessed. "My inventory is almost empty."

"We're going to have to craft our own potions now that Ilana is back in the real world," explained Michael.

Mr. Anarchy delivered some good news. "I have a command block in my inventory. I'd like to experiment with it now. One of us will get to leave the server. If it works, once we get more command blocks, we can go back to town and get everyone off, and we won't have to worry about Pablo and these attacks from the Ender Dragon."

"I think Blossom should go first since it didn't work when you tried the last time," Simon suggested.

"That's not fair," Blossom said. "I wouldn't feel right doing that."

"Really?" Robin asked.

"Yes," Blossom replied. "After all we've been through together, I think we all deserve an equal shot at getting off this server."

"Should we write our names on a piece of paper and place it on the ground like we've done in the past?" asked Michael.

"Yes, let's do that," Mr. Anarchy said.

Everyone wrote their name on a slip of paper and dropped it on the ground. Mr. Anarchy picked one up and called out, "Blossom. I guess the universe wants you to go."

Blossom smiled. "When I get back home, I promise I will try to get on to this server and work with you guys to get you off here and stop Pablo."

Robin thanked her friend. "I know being stuck on this server has been hard for all of us, but I'm grateful I met people like you, Blossom. You've really helped me."

Blossom searched through her inventory. "I want to give you my snowballs to help you battle the Ender Dragon."

"Oh no," Mr. Anarchy stuttered, "I c-can't stop the lightning bolt."

Before Blossom could hand over her snowballs, Mr. Anarchy's lightning bolt struck Blossom and she vanished with all of the snowballs.

"It worked!" Robin exclaimed.

The sounds of joy were quickly replaced with panic when a loud roar boomed through the jungle.

"Not again!" Robin cried out.

"And now we don't have any snowballs to throw at the Ender Dragon," Simon exclaimed.

Michael had taken out his pickaxe and was cutting down a large redwood tree. Simon looked over at him and asked, "What are you doing?"

"I have a plan!" Michael stated.

Robin and Mr. Anarchy were warding off attacks from the Ender Dragon by pounding into the beast with a barrage of arrows. The dragon was losing energy, but was still strong enough to plow its grey scaly wing into the two of them.

Michael called out, "Let's head to the river."

Robin was shocked when she spotted Michael carrying boats to the shoreline. She asked, "Are those boats to help us escape?"

"This will induce the Ender Dragon to follow us to the cold biome. We will have a better chance of fighting him there," Michael explained.

Robin, Mr. Anarchy, and Simon followed him to the water and hopped on the boats as the enormous dragon flew above them, trailing them to the cold biome.

The dragon lunged at Michael's boat, throwing him overboard.

"Michael!" Robin cried out when she looked down at the blue water and couldn't spot her friend.

"I hope he has a potion for breathing underwater," Simon said, as he aimed his arrow at the beast that flew above their boats.

"This is a nutty plan," Mr. Anarchy said, "but I really hope it works."

"I hope Michael is okay," Simon cried as he shot another arrow at the Ender Dragon and it exploded.

"Now we're escaping from nothing," Robin said with annoyance. "We could be back in Lisimi Village helping everyone make a grand escape from this server."

"But I still need a few more command blocks," Mr. Anarchy reminded them.

"I doubt we'll find any in the cold biome." Robin was exhausted and had little interest in stocking up on snowballs in the cold biome. "If only Blossom had been able to leave the contents of her inventory we wouldn't have to deal with all of this."

"But she couldn't." Mr. Anarchy felt guilty; he had summoned the lightning bolt too quickly. "It's my fault."

"No, it isn't," Robin said, "I don't want to place blame on you."

"I'm worried about Michael," Simon said as he stared at the empty boat floating in the water next to their boats.

"I know, me too," Mr. Anarchy agreed. "I hope he's okay."

Robin spotted large snowcapped mountains in the distance. "Snow! I see the cold biome!"

Simon exclaimed, "Michael! I see Michael on the shore."

Michael stood smiling on the snowy shoreline. He clutched a snowball in one hand and wore a large grin. "Welcome!" he hollered to his friends.

12
SNOW DAY

Robin climbed out of the boat onto the icy ground. "I have to admit, it's pretty here. I'm glad I got to see this biome one last time before we left. It's definitely different when you're visiting here in a game and when you're actually *trapped* in the game."

"I agree," Michael said and playfully threw a snowball at Robin. She quickly retaliated and flung a snowball back at Michael, prompting the gang into a snowball fight.

Giggles were heard and the gang enjoyed a good old-fashioned snowball fight, until Lily appeared.

"Lily!" Michael threw a snowball at her and laughed.

"I'd love to play, but you guys have to get busy and gather snowballs. This is no time for joking around. I don't trust Pablo at all, and I fear he'll shut down this server and destroy you guys."

"What?" Mr. Anarchy was stunned. Despite once being a master griefer who had issued many empty threats, he had never threatened to destroy the server. His heart started to pound. He didn't want to be wiped from existence. "What about Fred the Farmer?"

"And Juan the Butcher?" asked Simon.

"And Emily the Fisherwoman . . ." Mr. Anarchy finished. "They'll all be gone forever if Pablo destroys the server!"

"If you get off the server, Pablo will have no reason to attack and destroy this server," explained Lily. "Just concentrate and get off of here as quickly as you can."

The gang halted the fight and gathered as many snowballs as they could fit in their inventories. Lily joined her friends, but excused herself when her mother needed to use the computer. She promised that she'd return and help them battle the Ender Dragon and defeat Pablo. Then she added, "But I hope I see you guys in the real world first."

"Me too," Simon said as he filled up his inventory with snowballs.

"My inventory is almost full," Robin said. "Unfortunately all I have are snowballs. I have no potions left."

"I don't have any potions either," Simon noted after he perused his inventory.

"What are we going to do?" asked Michael.

Mr. Anarchy asked everyone what ingredients they had in their inventories. "We can brew some," he suggested.

As the group discussed what ingredients they were missing, Lily reappeared. Robin exclaimed, "You're back!"

"I forgot to tell you guys that I know where you can get some command blocks," Lily said.

"Where?" asked Robin.

"I know there are some in a Nether fortress," Lily replied.

"How do you know this?" questioned Michael.

"I saw them," she said, "and I'd get them for you but I have to get off the server now." With that comment, Lily disappeared.

"The command blocks are in the Nether," Michael moaned.

"That's good, we need to go there. We are in desperate need of supplies for brewing potions. If we can do a quick trip to the Nether, we can get everything we need and head back to Lisimi Village and prepare to make our way back to the real world," said Mr. Anarchy.

"I wish I could see things the way you do," Robin sighed. "I really hate the Nether. It's creepy and way too challenging."

"Nobody likes the Nether," explained Mr. Anarchy, "but we must make this one trip in order to save everyone and ourselves."

"Okay, I'm in." Robin took a deep breath as she placed obsidian down on the snowy ground. "I don't have enough to craft a portal," she stated. Robin searched through the inventory hoping she'd find more obsidian, but there simply wasn't any more.

Michael called out, "I'm out of obsidian."

Simon also didn't have any obsidian. "What about you, Mr. Anarchy?"

"I don't have any either." Mr. Anarchy was upset. "What are we going to do? We have to get to the Nether."

Pablo appeared and asked, "What's the matter?"

"We aren't telling you." Robin leaped at Pablo with her diamond sword, but knew it was pointless to battle him.

"I don't understand why you think I'm a bad guy," Pablo said. "I'm not. I'm here to help."

Robin shouted at Pablo, but everyone told her to calm down.

Mr. Anarchy knew Pablo might have obsidian on him, but he didn't want Pablo knowing their plans. He had a serious internal debate, weighing the pros and cons of admitting that they were traveling to the Nether. If Pablo were intent on destroying them, thought Mr. Anarchy, he would destroy them no matter what. Mr. Anarchy then reasoned that Pablo could see the portion of the Nether portal that lay on the icy ground, so there was no use hiding their trip to the Nether. Mr. Anarchy decided to ask their potential enemy for help. "Do you have obsidian?"

"Yes, I do," Pablo replied as he placed his obsidian next to the other blocks on the ground, making a rectangular shape. He ignited the portal for the group. The gang hopped on the portal. As purple mist surrounded them, they watched Pablo laugh and disappear.

13
NEVER IN THE NETHER

"**W**here did Pablo go?" Robin questioned, "and what is he planning for us?"

"We can't worry about that." Mr. Anarchy pointed at a group of white ghasts that darted across the sky toward them. "We have to destroy these ghasts."

Robin looked up as the ghasts unleashed high-pitched sounds and shot fireballs. Robin used her fist to deflect one fireball, striking the ghast and destroying it. She was confident that she would win this battle. However, when she was struck by a fireball and lost a heart, she was humbled and quickly called for help.

Michael, Simon, and Mr. Anarchy used a combination of snowballs, arrows, and their fists to help Robin destroy the white flying fiery mobs.

When the last ghast was destroyed, Robin gathered the ghast tears that had dropped. "Ghast tears are very valuable. We can use these to brew potions of regeneration."

"And other potions, too," Simon reminded her.

Michael called out as he spotted a Nether fortress in the distance. "We have to travel to that fortress."

The gang dashed past a couple of zombie pig-men and avoided making eye contact with them, as they navigated their way toward the luminous Nether fortress.

A group of blazes guarded the fortress, and the gang shot arrows at the flying mob until they were destroyed, but one of the blaze fireballs hit Mr. Anarchy, leaving his health bar dangerously low.

Robin handed him milk, and he took a quick sip, eyeing the sky for other powerful mobs that had the potential to destroy him.

Robin was the first to enter the fortress after she gathered netherrack from the side of the stairs. The others joined her and picked the remaining netherrack. Simon stopped and pulled his diamond sword from his inventory. Suddenly, he heard a noise. "Does anyone hear that bouncing sound?"

"Magma cubes!" Robin called out.

Simon leaped at the cubes, slicing one in half, while Robin clobbered the halved cube alongside Simon.

More cubes bounced toward them and the gang stabbed them with their swords. Robin called out in pain as she felt a sword slam into her back. She turned around and gasped as two wither skeletons lunged at her. Robin was sandwiched between the magma cubes and the wither skeletons. She didn't have any potions in her inventory and barely enough milk to make a proper recovery. She tried to fight back, as her friends came to her aid, but it was too late; Robin was destroyed. She respawned in her bed in the jungle and looked at the other bed for Mr. Anarchy. She wanted to TP back to the Nether, but she really didn't want to go there, and in any case, TPing to the Nether was impossible.

Mr. Anarchy spawned in the bed next to her.

"Mr. Anarchy!" she called out. "You're back!"

"Yes," he spoke quickly. "We have to TP to Lisimi Village. I have the command blocks and we must get everyone off this server as soon as possible. I think Pablo is ready to destroy it."

Robin didn't ask questions; she followed Mr. Anarchy back to Lisimi Village and gathered the townspeople.

"Everyone! Meet in the center of town! We're going home!" Robin exclaimed.

Michael and Simon stood outside Mr. Anarchy's lab and asked each person to write their name on a slip of paper.

Juan rushed over and gave a thumbs up, "You guys are back! I'm so happy to see you and to be able to say good-bye."

A townsperson cried out in alarm, "A skeleton!"

Robin looked up at the sky. Night was approaching and it was dark enough for skeletons to spawn. She announced, "We will leave first thing in the morning. It's too dangerous to leave now."

Mr. Anarchy bolted from his lab. "Who gave you the power to make that decision?" he shouted at Robin.

At that moment, the townspeople fled to their houses as an army of skeletons invaded Lisimi Village.

Robin pointed to the endless sea of skeletons and replied, "They did."

Michael cried, "We have to brew those potions."

"This isn't the best time for making potions," Simon retorted as he battled three skeletons.

Lily reappeared, to their relief, and doused all of the skeletons with potions, weakening the entire army.

Everyone slammed their swords and arrows into the bony beasts until the final skeleton was destroyed.

"Can we wait until morning? Or do we have to leave now?" Mr. Anarchy looked at Lily. He needed answers.

"You can wait until morning, but you must get out of here the minute the sun rises," she warned them.

"We will," Mr. Anarchy promised. Lily vanished.

The names of the townspeople littered the ground. Everyone headed back to their home, wondering who would be the first to be chosen in the morning.

14
GOOD-BYE AND GOOD LUCK

The sun had just come up and already a crowd had gathered in front of Mr. Anarchy's lab. Everyone couldn't wait to leave the server. Michael checked with Mr. Anarchy and asked if he should pick the first name.

"Yes," Mr. Anarchy called out from his lab. "I will summon the first lightning bolt."

The assembled villagers were chatting and everyone could feel the excitement emanating from the incredibly energetic crowd.

Michael announced, "We are picking the first person now." He leaned down and picked up a slip of paper.

"Cassie," he called out.

A woman with red hair in ponytails squealed with happiness. "That's me! I'm here!"

The sky grew cloudy as a lightning bolt flashed through the sky and Cassie disappeared.

"It worked!" Michael exclaimed.

"Pick another name," people shouted from the crowd.

Juan, Emily, and Fred rushed over to watch each villager get zapped back to the real world. Juan said, "I can't believe this day is finally here. I'm so happy for all of you. I hope you come back on this server as a player."

Everyone promised they'd return. Michael picked another name from the ground and read it aloud: "Paul."

A man in a black suit stepped out from the crowd and shouted, "I'm ready!"

The second lightning bolt struck Paul, transporting him back to the real world.

Michael picked up another piece of paper and read it out loud, "Robin."

Robin was conflicted. She didn't want to leave her friends behind and felt it was her responsibility to see all the townspeople escape from the server. "Maybe I should put my name back on the ground," she suggested.

"Nonsense," Michael stated. He assured his friend she should seize this opportunity and leave the server.

Robin was about to decide when she heard a deafening roar and looked up at the sky.

"The Ender Dragon!" she cried.

"Get the snowballs!" Michael grabbed a couple from his inventory and pounded them against the dragon's side.

Simon and Robin aimed their snowballs at the powerful dragon. The townspeople helped battle the dragon. Everyone wanted this beast to be annihilated so they could leave the server fast.

Robin threw a snowball at the Ender Dragon. The icy ball hit the dragon's face, infuriating the lethal beast. Its red eyes stared intently at Robin as its muscular body flew toward her. Robin tried to duck, but she couldn't hide from the dragon. With no potions in her inventory and grasping just a snowball, she was powerless. The beast sped up as it lunged at her. She lost a heart. Robin tried to escape and dodge away from the dragon, but she was trapped. There was no escape. The dragon repeatedly swung at her until she was destroyed. Robin respawned in the cottage, and left her house ready to battle this tricky troublemaker. Snowballs shot through the air, but the dragon wasn't weakening.

Robin charged straight at the dragon because she wanted to be the one who annihilated the beast. She grabbed a snowball, but as she aimed at the Ender Dragon, it locked eyes with her and flew at her. She fell back and was destroyed again, and respawned in her bed.

Simon and Michael called out to Robin, as they continued to deplete their inventories of snowballs in the battle against this incredibly strong dragon.

"I've never encountered a dragon quite this powerful before," Michael stated breathlessly.

"Me neither," Simon agreed.

Mr. Anarchy used his last snowball. "I can't believe I've gone through my entire inventory."

"I only have a couple of snowballs left," Michael said. He was worried.

Robin hurried to rejoin her friends and threw a snowball at the dragon. Again, the cold ball hit the dragon's face and it roared in anger.

"It looks like that snowball actually made a dent in the dragon's health bar," Simon said. "We just need to hit it a few more times and we should be able to destroy it."

Robin quickly grabbed an armload of snowballs and heaved them at the dragon. She held one in each fist and aimed carefully.

Light emanated from the dragon's belly as the beast dropped an egg. Just as Robin reached over to grab the egg, Michael screamed, "Watch out!"

Robin had fallen into the portal to the End and disappeared.

15
IT CAN'T BE THE END

mr. Anarchy gasped, "We have to go after her!"

Michael, Simon, and Mr. Anarchy jumped into the portal before it faded.

"Robin!" Michael called out as he stood on a pillar in the dark and creepy End. A cluster of block-carrying Endermen marched in the distance.

The trio knew it was important to avoid making eye contact with any Enderman. An attack from an Enderman, with the Ender Dragon looming above them, would prove fatal.

"Watch out!" Simon warned the others. The Ender Dragon eyed the gang. The flying beast was extremely powerful in the End because it could replenish its health bar with Ender crystals, unlike in the Overworld, where the beast was a lot easier to defeat.

The dragon peered at the gang with its menacing red eyes. Simon grabbed a snowball and aimed for the Ender Dragon. The snowball landed on the dragon's side and its health bar diminished.

Roar!

The Ender Dragon leaped swiftly at the gang, focusing on Michael, who thought he was safely hidden behind a pillar.

Simon slammed his sword into the dragon and it plowed into Michael. As Simon struck the beast a second time, it unleashed another sonic roar and attacked him, too. Simon lost two hearts but was able to stab the dragon a few more times, weakening the beast.

Roar!

The infuriated dragon flew toward the Ender crystals, but Mr. Anarchy's arrow was aimed at the crystals and he struck and destroyed them right before the dragon had a chance to eat the energizing crystals.

"Help!" a voice cried out.

As Michael sipped milk, he heard Robin's cries. He looked around for her, but couldn't find her. The End was very dark and it was hard to see anything. The Endermen were still walking on the dimly lit floating island, and Michael feared making eye contact with the lanky mob. Endermites crawled on the ground next to the Endermen, and Michael knew he'd have to overcome numerous obstacles searching for Robin, but he had to do it.

"Help," the voice called out again.

Michael turned around, but he didn't see the Ender Dragon swoop down at him, knocking his energy bar.

He barely had enough strength to grab a sword from his inventory. Michael tried to strike the Ender Dragon, but he was destroyed first.

Meanwhile, Simon and Mr. Anarchy were too busy destroying the Ender crystals and battling with the dragon to hear Robin's cries.

"We just have to destroy the Ender crystals," Simon called to his friend who was slamming snowballs into the powerful dragon.

Mr. Anarchy heard a faint cry in the distance. "I think I hear Robin now," he told Simon, but Simon paid no attention.

Simon concentrated hard as he shot an arrow at the last remaining Ender crystal. "Got it!" he shouted.

Simon rushed over to Mr. Anarchy carrying a handful of snowballs and began throwing them at the dragon.

Mr. Anarchy exclaimed, "I hear Robin. She is crying for help."

"We can't find her until we destroy the dragon," Simon reminded him as they continued to pound the dragon with icy cold snowballs.

The dragon was growing weaker and angrier. It let out a deafening roar, drawing the attention of the cluster of Endermen walking on the floating island. One of the Endermen locked eyes with Simon. It shrieked and teleported to Simon. With a snowball in one hand and his diamond sword in the other, Simon skillfully annihilated the Enderman and was even able to strike the Ender Dragon.

"Help!" the voice called out again. This time it was louder.

"Robin," Mr. Anarchy yelled, "we're over here. We're battling the Ender Dragon."

Simon let out a sigh of relief when the other Endermen didn't seem to notice him. He grabbed another snowball from his inventory and when he went to get another, he noticed there were only two more snowballs remaining. "I'm running low."

"Me too," Mr. Anarchy said nervously.

"Help," Robin cried.

Mr. Anarchy called out again, "Over here! Robin!"

Robin was battling Endermen and Endermites. She repeatedly slammed her sword into the Endermen and the Endermites, but the battle was quickly depleting her energy supply. She could see her two friends in the distance and yearned to make her way back to them, but it seemed impossible. She felt guilty, as if this was all her fault because she had carelessly fallen into the End portal. With a couple of hearts left in her energy bar, Robin mustered up the strength to strike an Enderman until he was destroyed.

"I can help you," a voice called out.

Robin shrieked when she saw Pablo standing in front of her. "Leave me alone. You've caused so much damage. We would have been home by now if it were not for you."

"I can't use the computer for very long. I'm being punished," Pablo confessed.

"So you're bad in the real world, too? That's not a surprise," Robin was annoyed. She didn't want to talk to Pablo; she wanted to focus on defeating the Endermen and Endermites and helping her friends defeat the Ender Dragon.

"I did get in a lot of trouble at home. Also, Lily won't communicate with me on email, text, or chat. I feel awful. I just want you to know that I'm gone. I'm banned from the computer for a week. I shouldn't even be on here now, but I felt badly for what I did—" Pablo didn't finish his sentence. He simply disappeared.

Robin couldn't believe Pablo didn't even strike one of the Endermen as he made his confession. She needed the help. As Robin struck the final Enderman that attacked her, she hoped Pablo was being honest and wasn't playing tricks with her. With one last blow to the Enderman, she was free to find her friends. Robin ran toward the roar of the Ender Dragon.

"I'm here!" she called out to her friends. With renewed energy, she hit the Ender Dragon with her diamond sword and destroyed it. The trio teleported into another floating platform in the End, which was filled with plants and a large building.

"Oh, my!" Mr. Anarchy marveled, "we're in the End city!"

They entered a lavish tower.

"Watch out!" Robin shrieked as a blocky purple beast encased in a shell popped up and shot a projectile that unleashed white particles in the air. The gang luckily dodged it, but before they could strike back, the beast was safely in its shell.

"What is that?" Simon cried.

"A shulker," Mr. Anarchy replied. "It's a powerful mob and we have to destroy it."

Robin aimed her arrow at the shulker, ready for the secured mob to pop back up from its shell, but it wasn't moving.

Simon spotted a ship. "I've heard about these ships in the End. They're filled with countless treasures."

Mr. Anarchy grabbed an Ender pearl and stated, "If we throw this Ender pearl, we can get onto the ship."

Robin continued aiming her arrow at the shulker. "But we can't go on that ship. We have to go back to the Overworld and get everyone off this server." She explained that Pablo had returned and apologized, and his parents had punished him and he wouldn't be on the server. "This is our chance to get free."

Simon stared at the ship docked at the pier and lamented, "But we might never see a ship in the End again; this is a rare find."

"We need to get home," Robin reminded them. The shulker popped up and shot at her, but she aimed her arrow and destroyed the shulker.

Robin was annoyed at her friends when she saw them climbing onto the ship. Nevertheless, she followed them aboard. Robin's eyes widened as she gazed at the treasure that filled the ship. "Wow! This place is unreal." As the trio gathered treasure, Robin spotted another shulker. She was about to strike it when she heard a familiar voice call out.

"Lily!" Simon exclaimed.

"Get back to the Overworld right now and get off this server," Lily demanded and then disappeared.

16
FINAL RIDES

I t was morning and the sun was shining brightly on the village. Mr. Anarchy moved the command blocks to the center of Lisimi Land as everyone gathered near the blocks.

"Today is the day we all go back home!" Mr. Anarchy announced, and the crowd cheered.

"Let's have one last ride on the roller coaster," proposed Michael.

"Yes, we'll celebrate!" Simon agreed.

Everyone cheered.

Juan stood in front of the crowd and spoke: "I'm going to miss having you all in the town. But I do hope you come back as players, and I can chat with you at the butcher shop."

Fred the Farmer and Emily the Fisherwoman both admitted they'd also miss them and hoped they would return as players.

"Of course we will," Robin said with a smile.

Simon suggested, "We should empty our inventories and store them in chests, so we can have access to all of our stuff when we return."

"That sounds like a great idea," Robin remarked.

Mr. Anarchy said, "Maybe that explains why there were so many empty chests. I'll bet Pablo and his friends did the same thing, and when he returned he looted them."

"That makes sense," Michael said.

The townspeople emptied their inventories into chests and started to line up for the roller coaster.

Michael's smile grew when he spotted Lily. "I'm glad you're here."

"This is great! Everyone is getting off the server at last," she said.

"We're just going on one last ride on the roller coaster," he explained.

Lily watched the roller coaster fly by and sighed, "This is where it all began. If we hadn't been protecting this roller coaster, we never would have gotten trapped on this server."

"Would you like to ride on the coaster with me?" asked Michael.

"Of course!" Lily replied.

Michael and Lily rode the coaster with Simon. When the ride came to a stop, they indulged in one final feast with the villagers.

Juan offered everyone food, and the gang dined on meat, potatoes, and cake. Lily looked at Mr. Anarchy and said, "It's funny that you go by the name Mr. Anarchy. I've always wanted to know what your first name is."

Mr. Anarchy replied, "John. I always thought it was odd that you guys never asked."

The gang joked about Mr. Anarchy's name and everyone promised to meet up on the server as players.

"Now that we know how to get back on here, let's make sure to get together again," Michael told Robin.

"Yes, we will," Robin agreed.

Mr. Anarchy made his final announcement: "It's time for everyone to write their name on a piece of paper again. We have to pick who will get back to the real world."

Michael picked a paper off the ground. Robin was one of the first to leave. Even Mr. Anarchy's eyes swelled with tears as he said good-bye.

Simon was the last name chosen before Mr. Anarchy zapped himself off the server. Simon was jolted back to his parents' house in the middle of the storm.

"Simon!" his mother called out.

Simon raced down the stairs to the basement. He looked affectionately at his mom and realized how different he felt seeing her now. He had just spent almost a year living on his own in the world of Minecraft, but here he was back in his parents' house and he had to go to school the next day. A lump formed in his throat when he remembered he was in trouble with his teacher, Mrs. Sanders. Thunder boomed. The lights went out and Simon clutched the flashlight and let out a cry.

"It will be okay, Si," his mother reassured him. "It's just a storm. It will pass." Simon moved closer to his mom. She put her arm around him. Simon had missed this. There was no one around to comfort him when he was on the server. In Lisimi Village, it was all about survival. Simon couldn't believe the storm had so much power over him. He had slayed zombies, Endermen, the Wither, and countless other mobs, including the Ender Dragon, but felt himself trembling here on the floor of his basement. He wanted the storm to finish and the thunder to stop shaking the house. He could hear rattling from the large window in the living room.

"Is this a tornado, Mom?" Simon's voice quavered.

"No, just a bad storm that will stop soon. Everything will be okay," his mom replied and hugged him. He could feel the powerful wind blowing outside and wondered what his home would look like after the storm ended. He knew that, like in Lisimi Village, he could rebuild. Simon sat in the dark basement and thought about all of his friends in Lisimi Village. He hoped he'd be able to meet up with them on the server. It was devastating to think he'd never see them again.

The storm passed and Simon and his mother cautiously made their way back up the dark basement stairs. Simon's first instinct was to log on to the computer, but he knew he had to help his mom. Only one window was shattered and as they cleaned up the pieces of glass, he could see Michael and his mom walking outside their home.

"Michael!" Simon exclaimed.

"Wow," his mother remarked, "you're so excited to see your friend! You just saw him in school an hour ago."

17
SERVERS

"**A**re you there?" Simon typed. He held his breath, hoping he'd see Robin's name.

"I'm here," Robin replied.

"You're back?" Juan the Butcher roamed the village streets announcing, "They're back!"

"We're all here," Lily informed him. "We're going to spend the day in Lisimi Land and then go on a large treasure hunt."

"We have to go back to the End," Simon said. "It was fantastic. I've never seen treasure like that before. We were in this amazing ship and it was filled with treasure."

"The End," Robin said thoughtfully and paused. "I would go back there, but not today. That's a huge undertaking."

Blossom appeared on the server and everyone cheered. Lily said, "I'm so glad you were able to find your way back here."

"And look who I brought with me!" Blossom grinned and pointed to Sunny.

"Hi, Sunny," Lily said.

The gang was happy to be reunited and walked together through the entrance to Lisimi Land. Lily asked each of her friends, "What was the first thing you did when you got back home?"

"I ate a chocolate bar," said Michael.

"I had pizza," replied Simon.

"I watched TV," confessed Lily.

"I went outside and played with my dog," said Sunny.

The gang was grateful be a part of both worlds now. Everyone was ready to hop on the roller coaster when they spotted Pablo.

"What are you doing here?" Simon dashed over to Pablo and pointed his diamond sword at him.

"I came here to say I'm sorry." Pablo's eyes filled with tears when he admitted, "I miss you guys. I was awful."

Simon looked around at the others. He wasn't sure if they should forgive Pablo.

Mr. Anarchy surprised everyone when he walked right over to Pablo.

He said, "I know you feel badly, but I think you should stick to another server. We want this one to be fun and we don't want any griefers."

"How can you say that?" Pablo grumbled, "You are the reason everyone was trapped on here. If they could forgive you, how come they can't forgive me?"

Mr. Anarchy understood Pablo's point. He stood by him silently. Simon stepped between the two and said, "I think Mr. Anarchy has proven his dedication to us. So you can stay on this server if you can prove that you are a team player and not someone who likes to create trouble."

Lily added, "We like people to have opinions and enjoy playing the game, but we don't want someone who will make us feel threatened, and that's what you did. You made us feel very scared and threatened."

Pablo looked down at his feet as he spoke. "I'm sorry I made you feel that way. This past week I wasn't allowed on the computer and I had a lot of time to think. I realized that I wasn't very nice to you guys and if you let me stick around here, I promise I will make it up to you."

The gang allowed Pablo to stay. He rode all the rides with everyone at the amusement park and joined them on a treasure hunt.

It was almost nighttime and Simon suggested they all wrap up their day on the server and head back to the real world.

"I'd like to sleep in my bed in the cottage. I miss it," said Lily.

The others agreed. They missed their homes in Lisimi Village, and they hurried back home to avoid any attacks by hostile mobs.

As Lily crawled into bed in the cottage, she looked at Robin. "This is fun. I love knowing we can shut the game off at anytime."

"Me too," Robin said with a smile and drifted off to sleep.

18
NEW STUDENT

"I can't believe we're back at school," Simon said as he stood at the entrance to the school.

"You'd better not pass any notes today," Lily joked.

"I won't," Simon replied with a grin.

The duo walked into the classroom and took their seats. Lily felt like she hadn't been in the classroom in ages, and she hoped she would remember how to do fractions. She looked inside her desk and leafed through a book she had been reading. She knew she'd have to start it over from the beginning. Her memory of the last lesson at school was foggy. She mostly remembered Simon getting in trouble.

Mrs. Sanders said, "I want everyone to leave their homework on their desk, and I will come around and check it."

Homework! Lily's heart raced. She wasn't sure she had it. She rummaged through her backpack and let out a sigh of relief when she spotted the worksheet in her folder. She had done her homework. It just seemed like years ago.

"Good job, Lily," Mrs. Sanders said and picked up Lily's worksheet.

Lily glanced over at Simon and Michael who also had the worksheets on their desks and smiled. She was happy they were all prepared for school. It was going to be a tough adjustment, though.

At recess, Lily chatted with Simon and Michael.

"I think coming back is harder than we imagined," confessed Lily.

"I wonder how the others are doing," Michael said.

"I know," Lily replied. "At least we have each other. I'd be lost if I was adjusting to school alone like Robin did."

Michael saw Mrs. Sanders walk a boy in a blue jacket over to a group of kids playing soccer and introduce him. He could hear other kids whispering about the new boy, "Who is that kid? When did he start here?"

"I think he's going to be in our class," Lily said. "I overheard Mrs. Sanders talking about it. He just moved here from another town."

They looked over at the new kid as he took his blue jacket off to play the game. Simon said, "Look! He's wearing the same Minecraft shirt as me."

Lily joked, "That's not too difficult. You own a ton of Minecraft T-shirts."

"We should talk to him about the game," said Simon.

"Maybe after school," Lily said as the recess bell went off and they headed back into class.

Mrs. Sanders stood in front of the class with the new boy. "Since we all sit alphabetically, you will sit next to Michael. Michael, please introduce yourself."

"Hi, I am Michael Andrews," Michael said with a smile.

"Hi, I am John," said the new kid. "John Anarchy."

DO YOU LIKE FICTION FOR MINECRAFTERS?

Read the
Unofficial Minecrafters Academy series!

Zombie Invasion
WINTER MORGAN

Skeleton Battle
WINTER MORGAN

Battle in the
Overworld
WINTER MORGAN

Available wherever books are sold!